THE UND

Tyndale House books by Tim LaHaye and Jerry B. Jenkins

The Left Behind series
Left Behind
Tribulation Force
Nicolae
Soul Harvest
Apollyon
Assassins
Book 7 available spring 2000

Left Behind: The Kids
#1: The Vanishings
#2: Second Chance
#3: Through the Flames
#4: Facing the Future
#5: Nicolae High
#6: The Underground

Tyndale House books by Tim LaHaye
How to Be Happy though Married
Spirit-Controlled Temperament
Transformed Temperaments
Why You Act the Way You Do

Tyndale House books by Jerry Jenkins
And Then Came You
As You Leave Home
Still the One

The Underground 6

LEFT BEHIND™
>THE KIDS<

Jerry B. Jenkins

Tim LaHaye

WITH CHRIS FABRY

TYNDALE
KIDS

TYNDALE HOUSE PUBLISHERS, INC.
WHEATON, ILLINOIS

To Erin

TABLE OF CONTENTS

What's Gone On Before ix

1. Word Power 1

2. Deadline Countdown 13

3. The Crash 25

4. Delivery Day 35

5. Where's Vicki? 47

6. The Dangerous Plan 57

7. Breakthrough 69

8. A Friend for Ryan 81

9. Fugitives 93

10. Betrayed 103

   About the Authors 113

What's Gone On Before

JUDD Thompson Jr. and the other three kids living in his house have been involved in the adventure of a lifetime. They have been left alone without family after a global catastrophe.

Judd is the oldest at sixteen. Vicki Byrne, fourteen, and Lionel Washington, thirteen, have lost parents, brothers, and sisters. They are church kids so they know the truth immediately. Jesus Christ has returned to snatch away true Christians in the twinkling of an eye.

But Ryan Daley, twelve, and his parents didn't go to church. Ryan doesn't know where to turn when his parents are killed in the chaos.

The four kids stumble onto each other at the New Hope Village Church in their town of Mount Prospect, Illinois. All four dramatically come to believe the message Pastor Bruce Barnes gives them. They also learn what the Bible says about events that lie ahead.

Now school has begun. The Young Tribulation Force devises a plan to spread the news of God's love through an underground newspaper. But they will need wisdom and courage to withstand the enemies of God during the seven most chaotic years the planet will ever see.

ONE

Word Power

Vicki Byrne awoke with a start at 4 A.M. She could not push from her mind her friend Shelly. Vicki had prayed for Shelly often, but this morning was different. The more she thought of her, the more concerned she became. Was Shelly in some sort of danger?

Vicki wanted to talk to Shelly about God, but each time it was as if the door had closed. Either Shelly was busy or Shelly's friend had barged in and stopped the conversation. Vicki could tell Shelly was still in shock after the disappearances. Shelly needed the truth. Each time Vicki had called her, she either got the answering machine or someone who said Shelly couldn't talk right now. It would have been easy to give up and talk to people who wanted to hear her message, but Vicki couldn't get Shelly out of her mind. Shelly looked so lost and confused.

She dialed Shelly's number but hung up before it rang. *This is crazy! Her mom will kill me if I wake them up at this hour for nothing.*

She picked up her journal. "Please God," she wrote, "give me a chance to speak to Shelly about you today."

＊

At breakfast Judd told Lionel and Ryan, "Remember to be waiting for us after school today. I don't want to be late for our study with Bruce."

"Yes sir!" Ryan said, saluting. "By the flag-pole."

"Too many war movies," Lionel muttered, shaking his head.

"I'm not kidding," Judd said. "Don't be off playing soccer or basketball—"

"We'll be there," Lionel said, scowling at Ryan.

"My newspaper could be what God uses to get to students. Maybe they'll take it home to their parents."

Vicki squinted. Judd was talking as if it were his idea. She felt silly for caring. Couldn't she just be happy it was being done and that people would be reached? But Judd shouldn't care either.

"We get to help, right?" Ryan said.

"I need everybody," Judd said. "The school paper comes out on Tuesday. I want to beat them and get ours out Monday. Vicki and I will write the articles and get it on the computer, but we need you guys to help print and fold and—"

"Grunt work," Lionel said.

"There's no little job," Judd said. "We're starting with 500 copies. That'll take everybody's help."

"How are you gonna give it out?" Ryan said.

Judd shrugged. "I figure I'll take one entrance and Vicki can take another. We'll hand it out as the kids go in."

Ryan poked at his cereal and shook his head. "What if the principal and that coach, what's his name?"

"Handlesman," Vicki said.

"Yeah. What if they stop you before you get started?"

"He's right," Vicki said. "No Bibles, no talking about God, you know the drill. Everybody's scared."

"Distribution is the least of my worries right now," Judd said. "We need to write the *Underground* first."

"Is that what you're calling it?" Vicki said.

"Got a better idea?"

On the way to school Judd reminded Lionel and Ryan again to be ready after school. When they were gone, Vicki said, "You might want to go easy on them. I mean, you can come across wrong if you're not careful."

Judd cocked his head. "I want them to understand how important this is. You know how busy Bruce is, and we only have the weekend to get the paper done if we want to distribute it Monday."

Vicki didn't like having PE first thing every day. Mrs. Waltonen sometimes lost track of time, and they were barely able to dress before second period.

"Byrne!" Mrs. Waltonen shouted as the class ended.

Vicki ran over as the other girls left the gym. Thin and dark with short hair and glasses, Mrs. Waltonen had seemed shattered the week before while talking about losing her grandchild in the disappearances.

"The other day," Mrs. Waltonen said, "you

said something about knowing where people were. The ones who disappeared."

Vicki nodded.

"You know I can't allow those conversations. About religious things."

"I don't want to offend anybody," Vicki said. "I won't disrupt class anymore, if that's what you mean."

"You don't understand," Mrs. Waltonen said, lowering her voice. "After class, on a personal basis, you know, one-on-one, I don't think they said anything about that."

"You want to talk about where your grandson is?"

"Granddaughter," Mrs. Waltonen said. "Not even six months old."

Vicki stared at the teacher. Mrs. Waltonen was older than Vicki's mother, and yet she was looking to Vicki for some kind of hope.

"Everybody's lost someone," Mrs. Waltonen said, "and it's left us without answers. But you're—well, better because of it. Something's different for you, Vicki."

Mrs. Waltonen suddenly seemed so soft. With her shrill whistle and the way she barked orders, she was the last person Vicki would have expected to start such a conversation.

"I *have* changed," Vicki said. "And the reason I believe I know about your—"

The bell rang. Girls ran from the dressing room.

"You have to go," Mrs. Waltonen said, touching Vicki's arm.

"It's OK. I want to stay and talk—"

"Maybe later. Maybe Monday."

Vicki didn't want to let the moment go, but Mrs. Waltonen urged her to dress and get to class. Vicki wondered if she would actually have the chance to lead one of her teachers to the truth.

Vicki was late for second period. She wiped her forehead and said, "I had gym." The teacher let it pass. After each class she looked for Shelly. She felt more than ever that something was wrong.

※

"A kid in homeroom got her Bible taken," Lionel said in the car after school. "They called it 'dangerous material.'"

"All we hear is stuff about self-esteem and peace," Ryan said. "Makes me sick."

Judd thought Bruce Barnes would be overjoyed at Vicki's news about talking with her PE teacher. But they found him weeping, his head on his desk. A young woman rose to meet them and closed Bruce's door.

"I'm Chloe Steele," she said. "You must be the Young Trib Force."

Judd, Vicki, and Lionel introduced themselves, but when Chloe saw Ryan, she hugged him tight. "I know you, don't I? You used to play with Raymie."

Ryan looked embarrassed and didn't seem to know what to do. "Raymie's her little brother," he explained.

"I'm sorry," Chloe said. "I'm helping in the office, and Pastor Barnes is not having a good day."

"What's wrong?" Judd said.

Before she could answer, the door opened and Bruce waved them inside. Judd saw tear-stained pages on Bruce's desk and recognized the church directory. He picked it up and saw Bruce, a bit younger and fuller in the face with a pasted-on smile. Surrounding him were his wife and children. What a treasure Bruce had lost!

On the next page was Dr. Vernon Billings, the now departed senior pastor. Judd quickly turned to the back of the directory and found his own family. His mother and father stood behind the smiling twins, Marc and Marcie. Judd was off to the side, a few inches from the rest, straight and rigid. No smile. He looked like he wanted to be anywhere but in that picture. Judd flipped through a few other listings and saw friends and familiar faces now gone.

"Let me see," Vicki said. Ryan pointed out Raymie's picture and then grew quiet. Bruce wiped his eyes.

Bruce explained that the reporter, Cameron Williams, had discovered the directory and was impressed by the pictures of the Steele family. Chloe blushed.

"It brought it all back to me," Bruce said. "All the pain that night my wife and kids were taken."

Bruce composed himself and asked if anyone minded if Chloe joined them. No one objected.

"There's been a development with the two witnesses in Jerusalem," Bruce said. Judd noticed the others sit straighter when they heard Bruce's solemn tone. "This is going to be on the news tonight, and you may not want to watch. A half dozen thugs tried to charge the witnesses. I don't know what they thought they could do, but they were killed. On the spot."

"What happened?" Judd said.

"They were burned to death."

Vicki gasped.

"Cool," Ryan said.

"There's nothing cool about it," Bruce said. "God judges his enemies. But you can bet this breaks his heart too. What you saw was a direct fulfillment of God's prophecy in Revelation 11. Grab a Bible and let's read what the angel tells the apostle John."

Bruce asked Vicki to read the passage.

"'"And I will give power to my two witnesses, and they will prophesy one thousand two hundred and sixty days, clothed in sackcloth." These are the two olive trees and the two lampstands standing before the God of the earth. And if anyone wants to harm them, fire proceeds from their mouth and devours their enemies. And if anyone wants to harm them, he must be killed in this manner.'"

For the next half hour Bruce explained this and other prophecies being fulfilled before their eyes. Vicki told of Mrs. Waltonen again and also how worried she was about Shelly. "Why wouldn't God let me see her today?" she said.

"I don't know," Bruce said. "But keep praying for her. Your chance will come."

The six of them huddled to pray and ask God for opportunities to speak of their faith. Bruce prayed that people would have their eyes opened to the truth.

Over hamburgers in front of the TV, Ryan said, "We forgot something."

"Don't talk with your mouth full," Lionel said. "I can see pickles. What'd we forget?"

"We didn't ask Bruce about the *Underground.*"

Judd smashed his trash and tossed up a shot that bounced around the can and dropped in. "*Ask* him?" he said. "Since when do we need Bruce's permission?"

"Judd!" Vicki said.

"I just think it would be better to surprise him," he said. "Let's get the first issue done and see what happens."

He didn't return Vicki's gaze. "I'm tired," she said. "I'll write my story in the morning."

Judd sat at the computer in his father's den. The next time he looked up it was 3 A.M. He still wasn't satisfied with the graphics for the *Underground* logo. Creating a newspaper was going to be a lot more difficult than he imagined.

He spotted a copy of the same church directory he had seen in Bruce's office. He leafed through until he came to his family. Judd had clenched his teeth hard at Bruce's office. He had to be strong. He had to be the leader.

What he wouldn't give to have his mom

and dad back! He wanted to ask questions. Life questions. Questions about the Bible. He missed his brother and sister. He just wanted to be with them and laugh again.

One picture haunted him. The youth group. All those kids sitting around a table, smiling and eating popcorn. Every one of them was now gone. All but one. All but him.

TWO

Deadline Countdown

By the time Judd awoke Saturday it was nearly noon, and he felt awful for sleeping so late. He showered and dressed and found the others waiting for him downstairs.

"Why didn't you guys wake me up?"

No one looked at him. They stared at a horrifying scene on CNN. A camera mounted high above the Wailing Wall showed two old men in robes below. From the left of the screen, six figures briskly walked forward.

"Watch this," Ryan said.

One of the men in robes—whom the kids knew to be the two witnesses prophesied in the Bible—lifted a hand while the other stood like a stone. As the group neared, fire flashed from the right of the screen and engulfed the six. Immediately the flaming men fell to the ground in a flailing heap.

"Oh, that's awful," Vicki said, turning away.

CNN showed the video again, this time enhancing the witnesses. The picture was blurry, but Judd could tell one man was talking, and then fire shot from the mouths of both. Vicki left the room.

"If you don't believe the Bible now," Lionel said, "you'll never believe it. That was exactly what we read in Revelation."

Judd turned off the television.

"Hey, I want to see that again!" Ryan said.

"This isn't a movie," Judd said. "Those were real people."

"I know," Ryan said. "I just want to see it one more time."

"Come on," Judd said, "I want to show you my newspaper."

Vicki was already in the den, staring at the screensaver. They gathered around the desk and Judd hit the mouse. A photo of Nicolae Carpathia High School appeared. Below it in bold letters: *The Underground*.

"Wow," Lionel said. "How'd you get the school's picture in there?"

"From a Web site of places recently named after Carpathia."

"Those are really cool letters too," Ryan said.

"It's new," Judd said. "I mixed a couple of fonts and finally got it right about 5 A.M."

Vicki crossed her arms but didn't speak.

"What do you think, Vick'?" Judd said.

"Uh—it's amazing. That took a lot of work. But—"

"What?" Judd assumed everyone would love what he had done.

"How are you going to print it? With all those colors, it'll take a long time, won't it? Shouldn't we go with something more low budget?"

Judd reddened. He wasn't about to see all his work go to waste.

"Why would you spend that much time on, well, the incidentals?" Vicki added.

"If you want people to read something," he said, "you have to put it in a nice package."

"But we can't physically print all that—"

"I don't want it to look cheap, like it came from some—"

"Trailer park?" Vicki said.

"No, I didn't mean that," Judd said. "Look, I'll figure it out. Just finish your article. I need to buy more supplies."

"I *am* finished. It's already on the computer." Vicki stepped in front of him. "You talk like the *Underground* was all your idea."

"Yeah," Ryan said. "You boss us around

like little kids, like we can't do anything. And you get to do *everything!*"

"I'm trying to do this right, so it'll reach the most people. If you don't like it, stay out of it."

"Fine by me," Ryan said.

"You can't admit you're wrong," Vicki said.

"I'll do it myself if I have to," Judd said. "Lionel, you in?"

"What do I get to do?"

"First we have to get a lot more paper and more printer cartridges. You want to go?"

It took Judd and Lionel an hour to select all the supplies. They rolled three full carts to the front of the store.

"Look at this," Lionel said, holding up a copy of *Global Weekly*. "It's got a blurb in here about Buck Williams's article on the disappearances. Can we get it?"

Judd paid for the supplies and magazine. The scene that afternoon had left him dazed. Because he was so determined, he got things done. But being headstrong made living and working with him difficult. It had always been this way. With his parents, with his little brother and sister, his way was the right way. Always had been.

"Lionel," Judd said as he drove home, "what do you think about Ryan and Vicki?"

"I don't know, man," Lionel said. "They

have a point. You were acting like king of the world this afternoon."

"I was tired. Anyway, they don't respect me."

"Hey, sometimes you have to earn respect. I mean, you don't like to be told what to do by Bruce, right? It's no different for us."

Judd sighed and shook his head. He thought when he became a Christian everything would be different. But he kept making the same mistakes. "I feel like a jerk," he said.

"You know what the Bible says," Lionel said. "First John 1:9 and all that."

Judd knew all right. He had memorized that verse as a little kid: "If we confess our sins, He is faithful and just to forgive us our sins and to cleanse us from all unrighteousness."

As soon as they unloaded the supplies into the house, Judd jogged up to his room and lay on the bed. "God," he prayed. "I can't do this on my own. I'm sorry. I didn't mean to hurt anybody. Please forgive me, and help the other kids to forgive me."

The house was silent when he came downstairs. Judd wondered if Vicki and Ryan had run away or were looking for another place to stay. He wanted to tell them he was sorry. He wanted the four of them to be a team again. But they were gone. Lionel was sprawled on the couch with the *Global Weekly.*

Judd wanted to grab readers and draw

them in with the first few words of his article. He played with the first sentence several times and finally decided on: "My life changed forever at 30,000 feet." He told his story anonymously. Running from his family, Judd had stolen and lied. Over the Atlantic Ocean, in a plane he should have never been on, the unthinkable happened. People all around him disappeared.

Judd described his return home and his discovery that his family was gone. The loneliness and hurt came back as he wrote. He hoped anyone reading the paper would feel the same and consider the truth he had found in the Bible.

"Judd, I have an idea," Lionel said. "*Global Weekly* gives a preview of Buck's article, but it says their Web site has an advanced look at it. What if we use some of this in the *Underground?* Is that legal?"

"We can find out later," Judd said. He set Lionel up on a different computer and let him work. Even if they didn't use Buck's report, it would keep Lionel busy.

✳

Vicki and Ryan kept walking. Vicki was upset about the blowup with Judd and knew Ryan was too.

"I don't understand it," Ryan said. "He can be your best friend, and then all of a sudden, bang, he turns into Dr. Jekyll. Or Mr. Hyde. Which was the bad guy?"

"Whatever," Vicki said.

"We ought to tell Bruce."

"What would he do—ground Judd? I don't think so."

"Somebody needs to talk to Judd."

They walked through half-empty neighborhoods. The farther they went, the bigger and more expensive the houses seemed to get. Vicki realized again how far she was from the life she had known.

"I'll bet the grass in these yards costs more than our trailer did," she said.

They came to a small lake with a playground and picnic tables. On a normal Saturday the beautiful park would have been filled with children running and playing. Now it was empty. There were no small children left.

"Do you ever stop missing them?" Ryan said.

"My family? I think about them all the time. On Saturdays my little sister used to ask me to play that memory game. You know, where you flip the cards over and try to get matches."

"I had one of those. It was animals. You

had to match the mothers with their babies. Kinda boring."

"That's what I said. I told her to leave me alone. She'd go into our room and play by herself or with Mom. I wish I had the chance—"

"I dreamed about my mom and dad the other night," Ryan said. "They were looking for me. I kept yelling at them, telling them where I was, but they couldn't hear me."

"I thought I heard somebody crying the other night," Vicki said.

"I try not to cry," Ryan said. "Sorry if I woke you up."

"It's not a problem," Vicki said. "I cry too."

"You do?"

"Yeah. And sometimes I just think about what might have been. What if I'd have believed what my family believed?"

"I've been praying that I could stop missing my mom and dad so much."

"I doubt you'll ever stop missing them," Vicki said. "But we could pray for each other that maybe it'll get easier with time."

Ryan looked embarrassed. "OK," he said.

A car passed slowly. Vicki wiped her eyes and shielded her face from the sun.

"What's the matter?" Ryan said.

"It can't be," Vicki said.

"That car?"

"Yes. It is!"

"Is what?" Ryan said.

"It's my gym teacher!"

Judd heard a car door and hurried downstairs. Vicki and Ryan quickly went to their rooms.

"Can we talk?" he called after them.

"What's to talk about?" Vicki shouted from downstairs.

Judd followed and stood awkwardly outside her door. Her room looked neat. And there was a hint of perfume.

"Who brought you home?" Judd said.

"I don't answer to you," Vicki said. "Go back to *your* paper and *your* ideas."

"Wait a minute," Judd said. "I need to say something."

"Say it," Vicki said.

"I want Ryan to be here too."

"Fine, let's go get him."

Vicki led the way into what looked like the aftermath of a tornado—socks and shirts everywhere, a half glass of milk on the nightstand, his bed a mess.

"Pretty neat about Vicki's gym teacher, huh?" Ryan said.

"Mrs. Waltonen brought you home?"

"You have a problem with that too?" Vicki said.

"As a matter of fact I do. Now she knows you don't live with family. Do you realize how dangerous that could be—for all of us?"

"I didn't tell her I lived here," Vicki said. "I told her it was a friend's house."

"Great, now you're in the clear and they're gonna come looking for me!"

"I'm not as dumb as you think I am," Vicki said.

"I don't think you're dumb, I just need you to understand that wasn't a very bright move."

"Something a trailer park girl would do, huh, Judd?" Vicki said. "For your information, Mrs. Waltonen asked about our church. She said she might come to hear Bruce tomorrow. She offered us a ride and I thought it would be a good chance to talk more. Satisfied?"

Judd sighed. Instead of getting better, things had gotten worse. He wanted to do the right thing, say the right thing, but everything came out wrong. Judd sat on the bed and rubbed his neck.

"I'm sorry. That's what I wanted to say. And about this afternoon, I was way out of line. Vicki, I did take credit for the idea, and I rolled over you guys like a bulldozer. I've been this way a long time, so it's not easy to change. I hope you'll forgive me."

Vicki and Ryan looked at the floor.

"Does that mean we're back on the *Underground?*" Ryan said.

"If you forgive me," Judd said. "And you'll be doing more than grunt work. I promise."

Vicki and Ryan smiled. It was more than Judd could have hoped for. The three bounded upstairs to the den where Lionel was still at work. Judd had already laid out his own article and started Vicki's on the second page.

"I like what you did, Vick'. It's a lot more personal than mine. If it's OK, I'd like to put Bible verses around the copy."

"Sounds good," Vicki said.

"You guys give me different verses, and we'll mix them with the articles. We can make them bold and put them in shaded boxes so they stand out."

"Maybe we could include the steps to knowing God that Bruce gave us," Lionel said. "You know, a prayer for salvation and stuff like that."

"Great idea," Judd said. "And we might use excerpts from the Buck Williams article in the second edition—that is, if we don't get caught and if there is a second one."

"How close are we to printing something

out?" Ryan said. "I want to see what it looks like."

"Tomorrow," Judd said. "By evening we should have the first issue ready to go."

※

At church the next morning Vicki looked all over for Mrs. Waltonen, but she wasn't there. Vicki didn't understand. She had so hoped the woman would be there.

At home Vicki herded Lionel and Ryan into the kitchen to get some lunch on the table. Suddenly she heard Judd scream, "Oh no!" She ran to the den and found him kneeling, his face on the floor.

"What happened?"

Judd sat up. She had never seen him this way. He looked pale and nauseated.

"It's gone," Judd said.

"What's gone?"

"The whole thing. Every word of it."

"What are you talking about?"

"The *Underground*," he said. "Everything we've done is gone."

THREE

The Crash

JUDD couldn't believe it. The screen was blank except for an error message. Each time he rebooted he got the same thing.

"Maybe it's a virus," he said. "I coulda picked it up off the Internet."

The four stared at the computer like it was a corpse.

"All that work," Judd said. "Gone."

"Did you save the articles and the logo on a separate disk?" Vicki said.

Judd shook his head.

"What do we do now?" Lionel said.

Judd pulled the computer tower from under his father's desk and looked at the connections. His dad had always said to check the little things. Make sure the monitor cable and power cords are tight. Everything was intact. But Judd noticed a silver sticker on the back that read: "Serviced by Donnie Moore." He dialed the number underneath.

"Oh, yeah," Mr. Moore said. "I installed that machine about six months ago. Fastest available at the time. Your dad paid big bucks for that box."

Judd read the error message to Donnie.

"Doesn't sound good," he said. "Let me finish a couple of things, and I'll be over in a half hour, OK?"

The kids ate lunch in silence. Judd felt like someone had kicked him in the stomach. He had wasted time and energy he could never replace. And the deadline approached.

"Any chance this guy can get the stuff back?" Ryan said.

"I doubt it."

"Know what I think?" Lionel said. "It's got something to do with the devil."

Vicki laughed. "That's crazy. What are we gonna do, ask Bruce to come over and cast demons out of the computer?"

"Think about it," Lionel said. "We're putting together an underground newspaper that hundreds of kids are going to read. Hundreds of kids who aren't Christians. Now if you were the devil, would you like that? Would you want all these people reading stuff about the Bible right when they're looking for answers?"

"He's got a point," Judd said.

"Yeah," Vicki said, "but don't pin everything on Satan. Maybe God didn't want that to be our first edition. Maybe *he* made the computer crash."

"How are we ever gonna know?" Ryan said.

"I think that's what faith is about," Judd said. "Remember the passage Bruce was talking about? The one about how things work together, something like that."

"I know!" Ryan said. He ran for a Bible and brought it to the table. Judd could tell he was excited. Ryan was the youngest and hadn't gone to church like the others, but he seemed to be absorbing Bruce's teaching like a sponge.

"Here it is," Ryan said. "Romans 8:28. 'And we know that all things work together for good to those who love God, to those who are the called according to His purpose.'"

"That's it," Judd said. "Not everything that happens is good, but God can turn it into something good."

"Even computer crashes," Vicki said.

Donnie Moore was in his late twenties, a blond with sideburns. Judd could tell he liked to talk. Donnie placed his hard-sided briefcase beside the tower and took the computer apart. As he poked inside, he told them about his business and his involvement with New Hope Village Church. He had installed phone systems and done odd jobs fixing printers and faxes for Pastor Billings and Loretta, the church secretary. But he had only attended church to expand his list of clients. His wife, Sandy, was interested in God and suggested they go. Though both heard a lot about the Bible, neither really changed. Except for Sunday mornings, Donny and Sandy lived the same as they had all their lives. After the vanishings, Donnie realized something about his belief in God was missing, but he wasn't sure what it was.

"I thought I just wasn't good enough," Donnie said. "The other people in the church were saints. They taught Sunday school, went to prayer meetings, and gave money to missionaries. They even let poor people sleep in the basement of the church and cooked meals for them. I thought I'd been passed by because I didn't have enough brownie points."

Donnie ran a diagnostic program as he continued.

"Then Bruce Barnes showed me the tape Pastor Billings had left. He explained what had happened to everybody. I'd never thought about God that way, the way your mom and dad must have, Judd. I found out I didn't have to earn my way to heaven, that Jesus had already paid my way by being perfect and dying in my place. All I had to do was receive the gift. I couldn't believe I had missed it so bad. 'Course even Bruce had made the same mistake. You too, I guess, hm?"

Donnie scowled at the screen.

"A virus?" Judd said.

"Nah, the hard drive. I mean, it could've been some kind of virus or maybe an electrical spike the surge protector couldn't handle, but whatever it was, it's fried. I was able to retrieve some of your dad's old files, but everything else is toast."

"Do we need a new computer?" Judd said.

"I don't see anything wrong with the rest of the box," Donnie said. "Just replace the hard drive and you'll be in business."

"How much do we owe you?" Judd said.

Donnie stopped at the door and put down his briefcase. "Your dad bought a service contract, so it's no problem. But I gotta ask you something. Do you kids know why this happened? Do you know what's going to happen?"

Vicki explained why they were so upset

about the computer crash. Donnie's eyes moistened. "Isn't that something?" he said. He was still shaking his head when he walked out.

*

"Plan B," Judd said that evening. "We're not letting this stop us. The *Underground* will be out in the morning."

"You gotta be kidding," Ryan said. "It took us three days to get this far. How are we going to start over and be done by tomorrow?"

"What are we gonna use, crayons?" Lionel said.

"We're going to use what's already been written," Judd said.

Lionel looked puzzled. "I thought everything on the computer was lost."

"We're using your words, Lionel. Yours and Buck Williams's. Did you finish it?"

"Yeah, but—"

"That's our first edition. We'll hook your computer to the printer, and we're on our way. Vicki, I know this is a long shot, but why don't you try getting in touch with Buck. He might be able to add something really powerful."

Buck was senior editor of the most prestigious newsmagazine in the world, so his article was a masterpiece. He covered every theory for the disappearances from UFOs and alien attacks to a cosmic evolutionary cleansing. But the middle of the piece interested the kids the most. Here Buck had included the truth. Jesus Christ had returned for true believers. Buck had interviewed several Christians, including an airline pilot the four figured was Rayford Steele. The Bible was communicated simply and powerfully.

"So we let the best journalist in the world write our first edition," Vicki said. "Perfect."

Vicki called Bruce for Buck's number, but he was reluctant to give it. Vicki said she wanted to ask some questions about his article, and Bruce gave her Buck's office number. His voice mail at *Global Weekly* gave his pager number. She left Judd's home number on his pager and was amazed when he called half an hour later.

"Using my stuff is a great idea," Buck said. "I didn't know it was on the Web yet. But don't quote me outside the article. Wouldn't be safe for me or you. Why not ask your questions and quote me as an unnamed source?"

"I'm really interested about what people from other churches think happened," Vicki said.

"Many Catholics are confused," Buck said. "While many disappeared, including the new pope, some remain. He stirred up a lot of controversy with a doctrine that seemed similar to the 'heresy' of Martin Luther."

"What was that?"

"Luther read the book of Romans and believed salvation wasn't gained through membership in the church, baptism, or doing good works. He said salvation was only by God's grace through faith. The new pope agreed with that, and it sent shock waves through the Catholic church.

"I talked with one of the leading archbishops, Peter Cardinal Mathews of Cincinnati. You might be hearing more from him in the coming months. Mathews said the vanishings were God's way of winnowing out the unfaithful. He compared it with the days of Noah when the good people remained and the evil were washed away."

"So he thinks we're the good guys and the people who vanished were bad?"

"Exactly," Buck said. "But remember, our view is that he was not a true believer. He was one who thought he could earn his way to heaven."

"What about the children and the babies?" Vicki said.

"He didn't have a good answer for that. He said he was leaving that to God."

Judd put Buck's anonymous quotes into a boxed article next to the text from *Global Weekly.* He and Vicki decided Ephesians 2:8-9 was the best passage to include there. It read, "For by grace you have been saved through faith, and that not of yourselves; it is the gift of God, not of works, lest anyone should boast."

By midnight the paper was done. It wasn't as professional as Judd wanted, and not as long, but it said what they all wanted to say. They printed and collated the pages as quickly as possible.

Vicki couldn't sleep. She had to be up in less than three hours for school. Her mind spun with fear and ideas. Might this be God's way of getting to Shelly? Would Vicki and the others be caught before even handing out the papers? If they did get the *Underground* to kids, would the kids actually read it? And what would the school do?

She put on her robe and went upstairs. Judd and Lionel were stacking the papers by the front door. Ryan was asleep in Judd's father's high-backed chair.

"I've been thinking," Vicki said. "This is bigger than all of us."

"I know," Judd said. "We couldn't have done this on our own."

The next morning in the car, Lionel pleaded with Judd. "Why can't we give out some copies at our school? Junior highers are just as important as older kids."

"I know," Judd said. "But this was written for high schoolers. If it works, we can do a version for you guys."

When they pulled up to Global Community Junior High, Ryan said, "Good luck. Or I mean, do it to it, or Godspeed, or whatever you're supposed to say."

Judd and Vicki waited until Ryan and Lionel ran into school before they laughed. Godspeed indeed.

FOUR

Delivery Day

Judd and Vicki carried the *Underground* in brown grocery bags. They tried to stay calm. Judd knew they concealed something school officials considered nuclear. Though they were early, many other students were already on campus.

"You know the plan," Judd said. "I'll meet you in the gym just before first period."

"Be careful," Vicki said. "It only takes one person to rat on us."

Vicki went toward the back entrance and Judd the front. He passed the flagpole and glanced up. Under the American colors was the white flag of peace with the school's new symbol, a dove. The words, "Nicolae Carpathia High School" flapped in the light breeze.

Judd focused on green newspaper bins by the front door. Students were to pick up anything placed in the bins. Newspapers, school memos, and even school-approved advertisements from local businesses were first come, first served. Everything had to be preapproved by the office, but Judd wasn't about to let anyone censor or throw out the *Underground*. They had worked too hard for that.

Four younger students stood talking near the bins, so Judd walked inside to the water fountain. When he looked again, the four were gone.

He shot back out the front doors and dropped the bag in the bin. He took a quick look around and ripped the bag open from top to bottom. The first copies of the *Underground* were exposed.

Judd hurried back inside to his locker. He fumbled with the combination, looking behind him. He believed no one had seen him, but he couldn't be sure.

Judd slid a few coins into a soda machine and took a drink back outside. He sat near the flagpole and watched the bins fifty yards away.

He took a sip of soda and thought about the kids in his old youth group. He had labeled them fanatics for standing around that very flagpole and praying. They had asked him to join them, and Judd just laughed. Now he knew how brave they had been to take a stand. He silently asked God for a chance to make up for the lost opportunity.

Judd froze when he saw a student walk to the door, do a double take, and grab a copy of the *Underground.* The boy placed it between his books and went inside.

A bus stopped in front of the school, and for a moment Judd couldn't see. He moved to get a better look and saw several students take copies. He was thrilled. Everything was going as planned.

Many kids who walked or drove to school used the rear entrance. Vicki wasn't scared of being seen by them. She could blend in. She was concerned about the faculty parking lot. Though they were supposed to be early, some teachers arrived later than students and bolted through the rear door. They stayed in their cars to smoke or listen to the radio until the last minute. Vicki watched the entrance. A group of kids was kicking a Hacky Sack between them. In the parking lot the principal, Mrs. Laverne Jenness, and one of the school secretaries got out of their cars.

When the kids saw Mrs. Jenness, they grabbed their books and ran inside. Perfect, Vicki thought.

Vicki walked toward the parking lot, then doubled back and followed the women. Once they were inside, Vicki stepped to the newspaper bins and poured out the papers.

She quickly folded the bag and turned to leave, nearly knocking someone over.

"Hey, watch where you're going," a man said. To her horror, Vicki found herself looking into the face of Coach Handlesman.

"Pay more attention, Red," Handlesman said.

Vicki hated that nickname. Usually she reprimanded anyone who called her that, young or old. But she bit her lip and forced a laugh.

"Sorry, coach."

Handlesman moved past her and picked up a paper on his way in. Vicki watched over her shoulder as she casually walked away. He stopped and looked like he was holding a dead fish.

"The *Underground?*" he muttered. "What in the world?"

Judd watched another bus pull up. He guessed that about every third student had taken the *Underground.* It was a start.

"God, don't let anyone get it who shouldn't."

Suddenly the front door burst open and Coach Handlesman ran out. He went directly to the green bins and grabbed the stack. He scanned the courtyard like a quarterback searching for a receiver.

Judd tipped his soda back and drained it, hoping Handlesman would be gone when he looked again. The coach could be on top of him in seconds. He drank the last drop. Handlesman was gone. So were all the copies of the *Underground*.

Vicki waited for Judd in the gym. A few kids were playing basketball. A couple at the back of the gym was making out. A group behind her passed something between them, but Vicki couldn't see what it was. When she saw Judd, she ran to meet him.

"Over here," Judd said, pulling Vicki underneath the bleachers. "What happened?"

Vicki told him. "I thought I was dead," she said.

"Didn't anybody take a copy back there?"

"Handlesman took one and then carted the whole bunch away. How about in front?"

"I'd say at least twenty got a copy. Maybe twenty-five, tops."

"We're going to have to think of some other way," Vicki said.

The PA system crackled in the gym.

"May I have your attention, students," Mrs. Jenness said. "Someone placed an unapproved newspaper in the distribution bins this morning. We believe most were confiscated, but if you picked up a copy thinking this was an approved publication, please bring it to the office immediately. It's called the *Underground*, and those caught with copies are subject to expulsion. Those behind these papers can avoid expulsion by coming forward now too."

"I can think of worse things than expulsion," Judd said.

Mrs. Jenness ended with, "There is a reward for anyone with information about those behind this newspaper."

"Great," Judd said. "Now there's a bounty on us."

Vicki heard movement overhead. "Judd, look," she whispered.

Judd said, "I see only feet and legs. What?"

Vicki pointed. "They're reading the *Underground*. Listen."

"Must be dirty or something," one girl said. "It'd have to be for them to make such a fuss."

"Shouldn't we turn it in?" another said.

"No. Read it. Pass it around."

"What kind of reward would we get?"

The first bell rang. Vicki shook her head.

"What's wrong?" Judd said.

"It was such a good idea. I just don't understand why God let Handlesman get most of the papers."

"I'm not discouraged," Judd said. "That

they were confiscated is a good sign. We're hitting a nerve."

"I wanted Shelly to get a copy."

"Maybe she did. We don't know. This just means we have to work harder. We have to be smarter now."

Vicki could think of nothing but the *Underground* all day. How would they get their message out now? Why didn't God let more kids see the paper?

Through the morning Vicki watched for signs of kids who might have seen the *Underground*. There were none. Mrs. Waltonen was nothing but business in gym class. Vicki wanted to ask her about Sunday, but Mrs. Waltonen went straight to her office after class.

Vicki's English teacher, Mr. Carlson, made a joke about the newspaper as class began.

"Anyone carrying any dangerous material today?" he said. "A copy of *Huck Finn,* a little *Catcher in the Rye*, some plutonium?"

The class laughed.

"Words are dangerous," Carlson continued. "Be careful how you use them. Some of the greatest writers in history have suffered because of their words."

"Are you saying whoever put out that newspaper was right?" a student asked.

"You have to take freedom of the press seriously," Mr. Carlson said. "But I doubt whoever's behind this paper compares to the great writers of literature."

Vicki wanted to say the Bible was the most censored book these days, and those who believed it were in the greatest danger. But she kept quiet.

At lunch Vicki couldn't find Judd. She ate alone and listened to her old friends at a nearby table. They ignored her, laughing and talking about their latest escapades. Vicki cringed. Was that what she used to be like? Did she brag about drinking and smoking and drugs? If only they knew the truth. Her life before Christ was empty. Listening to them now just made her feel sad.

She thought the day would never end. As she walked to her final class, a teacher stopped her.

"You need to go to the office immediately."

"What for?" Vicki said.

"It's an emergency. Something about a phone call from your mother."

Vicki gasped. Her mother was gone. Maybe Mrs. Jenness had discovered the truth and this was a trap.

She walked slowly to the office and found the secretary was the same woman she had seen with Mrs. Jenness that morning.

"Yes, you have an emergency call from your mother," the woman said. "You can take it over there."

Vicki picked up the phone. "I need to see you," a female voice whispered. "After school."

"OK," Vicki said tentatively. "Why?"

"Just get on your old school bus. Get off at your regular stop."

"I can't. I mean, I have something to do."

"You can and you will."

"You have to tell me what this is about before—"

"There were things in that paper today. You can help me—if you want to. Please."

The line went dead. Who would have known which bus she'd ridden? How did they connect her with the *Underground?* Was this a trap or an opportunity? She had to take the risk.

Judd paced in front of his car. Lionel and Ryan would be going crazy wondering where he and Vicki were. He had so much to tell her and ask her, but he couldn't find her. He walked into the school and past the office. No one was there except school employees.

As he walked back to his car, John and

Mark approached. They were the cousins he had noticed carrying Bibles the first day of school. Coach Handlesman had confiscated their Bibles.

"Judd," Mark said. "Big news on campus."

"What's that?" Judd said.

"The alternative newspaper. The *Underground*."

"I heard the announcement," Judd said.

"We worked on the school paper last year," John said. "They've changed it to the *Olive Branch* now. We stopped by the editorial office today to see how they're going to cover the *Underground* in tomorrow's issue."

"Did they have a copy?" Judd said.

"Not one," John said. "And since we're upstanding citizens, we turned ours into the office this morning."

Judd was concerned, then noticed the two were smiling. "You turned your copies in?"

"That's what they said to do," Mark said. "So we went to the library, made a few condensed copies for friends and acquaintances, and handed the original in to the principal."

"We follow the rules," John said. "And since the *Olive Branch* staff didn't have a copy, we made sure one wound up on top of the editor's desk."

"They probably won't be allowed to write

about the *Underground,* but it was worth a try," Mark said.

Judd leaned close. "Get in the car a second, guys. Have I got a story for you." John and Mark climbed in and seemed to drink in Judd's every word.

"Incredible," Mark said. "You guys sure know how to keep a secret."

"So," John said, "did you replace the hard drive?"

"Not yet. I need to buy one soon so we can do another edition."

"No need," John said. "We have everything at the house. Hard drives. Monitors. The huge ones. Our dad was a computer sales-man for the entire Midwest."

"How are you going to distribute another edition?" Mark said. "The school's gonna clamp down."

Judd shook his head and shrugged. "I knew it was going to get dangerous. Any ideas?"

John scratched his head. "I might have one. It's a long shot, and we'd have to put it together tonight."

"We?" Mark said.

"If Judd'll let us help."

"You're in," Judd said. "But what? How?"

"Believe it or not, we might be able to get

Nicolae High to distribute the *Underground* without even knowing it."

Judd took one more look around the school. Vicki was nowhere in sight.

FIVE

Where's Vicki?

AT dark there was still no word from Vicki.
Judd was frantic. He had taken John and
Mark to get their computer gear and raced
home, hoping to find her there. He found
only Lionel and Ryan waiting for answers
and not happy about having had to walk
home.

"Maybe the coach got her," Ryan said.

"I don't even want to think about that,"
Judd said.

"She'll be OK," Lionel said. "She can take
care of herself."

"I say we get Bruce to help us find her,"
Ryan said.

"Not yet," Judd said. "I'll give her another
hour."

John told Judd he was ready to get started
on the next issue. Mark wasn't so sure. "What
if we're caught?" he said. "What if Coach
Handlesman confronts you and asks you

point-blank if you had anything to do with the *Underground?* Would you lie?"

"Either God is in this or he isn't," Judd said. "If he wants us to do this, we gotta do it. He'll protect us. He'll give us the answers when we need them. We have to believe that."

"He either protects us or takes us to heaven," Ryan said. "Either way we can't lose."

"I'm not ready yet," Lionel said. "I mean, I want to be. I'd love to be a martyr, especially since I knew better and should have been ready for the Rapture, but I'm scared. I'm sorry, but I am."

The phone rang. As soon as Judd heard Bruce's voice he remembered their meeting.

"It totally slipped my mind," Judd said.

"Judd, we've talked about this before. My time is valuable. Please respect me enough to call and let me know the group's not going to be here."

Judd apologized again and set Thursday as their next meeting. "I promise we'll be there," he said.

Judd hung up, still worried sick about Vicki. Lionel had the floor. "In history today we talked about one of the big wars where a bunch of people were getting dragged away."

"World War II," Mark said. "The Nazis."

"Yeah, they came for the Jews and other people they didn't like, but some people couldn't stand what was happening and had to get involved. They hid Jewish people in attics and basements, wherever they could. I'll bet they lied to the Nazis. And they were right."

"If someone at school asks us directly," Mark said, "what are we going to do? You guys can talk about being brave, but when a teacher or Coach Handlesman is looking down at you, it's a different ball game."

"God doesn't need us to lie," Judd said. "But we also don't have to hang a sign around our necks that says, 'We're Christians, please persecute.'"

"Maybe we should do what Jesus did," Ryan said. "Bruce said the rulers asked Jesus questions before he was killed, and he didn't say *anything*."

"We're each going to have to decide for ourselves," Judd said. "We need to pray for wisdom. I don't know what the right thing is, but I do know one thing. We have to get this message out to as many people as possible."

Vicki had sat at the back of the bus. The trip took nearly half an hour, and no one talked to her. She guessed it was because she looked so different. No make-up. New clothes. She had hoped to sit near Shelly, maybe talk with her. But Shelly never showed.

The bus wound its way around apartment buildings and back streets. Finally she saw the familiar white roofs of the trailer park, and she moved to the front. She got off at her old stop with several others, then watched as they walked home. Except for empty lots where burned trailers had been moved, things looked the same.

Vicki waited, hearing nothing but traffic and muffled stereos and televisions. Then she heard a familiar voice behind her:

"Vick'."

She turned. "Shelly!"

Vicki threw her arms around Shelly, but Shelly's hug was halfhearted and she nearly lost her balance.

"It was you on the phone?" Vicki said.

Shelly nodded. "I figured it had to be good to get you out of class. So I was your mother for a minute. Pretty good plan for a girl like me, wouldn't you say?"

Shelly didn't seem right. She had acted spacey and distant the last time Vicki saw her. "Have you been drinking?" Vicki said.

"Who, me?"

"What is it, Shel'?"

Shelly looked at the ground. "I had to see you one more time. I wanted to say good-bye."

50

"You're leaving?" Vicki said.

"You could say that."

"Where are you going?"

"I picked up that paper today," Shelly said. "The one we weren't supposed to read. After lunch I hitched a ride home and looked through it."

Vicki couldn't believe Shelly had actually read the *Underground*. "What'd you think?"

Shelly touched her head. "I need to sit down."

"Let's go to your house," Vicki said.

"No," Shelly said. "My mom's in there."

Shelly collapsed and hit the ground hard, but instead of even wincing, she laughed. Vicki had seen this before. She didn't want to believe it.

"What did you take, Shelly?"

"I don't know what you mean."

"Shelly, tell me!"

"I don't know. Something of my mom's. Don't tell her. She'll really be mad."

"How much did you take?"

"The whole thing," Shelly said. "I don't want to be here anymore."

Shelly's eyes looked strange. Vicki grabbed her shoulders and Shelly's head lolled to one side.

"You were a good friend, Vick'."

"You hang on, Shelly, you hear me? Hang on!"

John and Mark knew what to do and had Judd's computer up and running in less than an hour. They were even able to retrieve the original file with the first newspaper, something not even Donnie Moore had been able to do.

"Cool logo," Mark said. "The file was damaged, but it can be fixed. I'd say the second edition is ready to print."

"How many can we distribute with your plan?" Judd said.

"Enrollment before the Rapture was about 2,300," John said. "I'd say we lost a quarter of that. Maybe 500 kids. I'd print 1,800 copies."

"You're kidding," Lionel said. "You can get the *Underground* to every kid without the school knowing?"

"If my plan works," John said.

Shelly's mother was lying on an old couch with the television blaring and hardly stirred when Vicki rushed in to call 9-1-1.

Paramedics began pumping Shelly's stomach in the ambulance. Vicki didn't know if she had gotten her friend to the hospital in time until a doctor came to her in the waiting room. "She's gonna be OK," he said. "She OD'd on sleeping pills. Shelly's lucky she had you as a friend."

Vicki glanced at a clock. 8:30. She ran to a phone.

"I'm really sorry, Judd," she said. "I'm at the hospital."

"What's wrong? Are you OK?"

"It's a long story. Could you pick me up?"

"I'll be right over."

Judd was upset, but he also cared. By the time he and Vicki returned to the house, he was frustrated.

"We need a signal," he said. "Some code that lets the others know one of us is in trouble."

"I couldn't get in touch with anybody," Vicki said.

"You don't need a code," John said. "You need this."

He pulled from his front pocket what looked like a pager. It had a screen about as thick as a pizza crust and was a little bigger than a watch.

"My dad was beta testing these," John said. "It works like a pager, but it's radio-frequency controlled. You enter a message on the screen and send it to whoever you want who has a receiver. Instantly. No phone calls, no modem."

"How much?" Judd said.

"We have at least ten more at home," John said.

Printing 1,800 copies of the *Underground* took all six kids. By midnight the papers were stacked and in the trunk of Judd's car.

John said, "We have a window of about an hour. We'll need to be there and ready by 4 A.M."

"I'm ready," Lionel said.

"No," Judd said. "You and Ryan aren't coming."

"No fair!" Ryan said.

"Judd," Mark said. "With 1,800 papers, we need their help."

Judd agreed, but only if everyone went to bed immediately. He set his alarm for 3:30 A.M.

The alarm woke Judd, but just barely. His body felt like lead. The others were slow to rise as well, except Lionel and Ryan. They seemed so excited Judd wondered if they had slept at all.

"Can you drop me off at the hospital afterward?" Vicki said.

"Sure," Judd said. "What are you gonna do about school?"

"I'll get there somehow. This is a lot more important than being late for class."

The six squeezed into Judd's car and drove across town. John gave instructions, and Mark briefed each on their assigned duties.

"Pull over here," John said. Judd parked in an alley and turned off his lights.

"The loading dock is over there," John said. "They put the finished papers for the school out a little after four o'clock."

At 4:10 A.M. a shaft of light came from the building as a man lugged three huge stacks and a smaller one onto the dock. He lit a cigarette and stood by the door.

"They get a break about now," Mark said. "He could be out here awhile."

"How do you know all this?" Lionel said.

"John and I worked on the school paper last year. We had pick-up duty. We got to know some of the guys on the dock."

Finally the man threw his cigarette on the ground and went inside. Judd pulled up to the dock. He opened the trunk and the Young Tribulation Force put their plan into action. If successful, the truth about the disappearances would be available to every student in their school.

SIX

The Dangerous Plan

JUDD found John and Mark's plan ingenious. They tucked a copy of the *Underground* inside each school newspaper. When a student grabbed a copy of the *Olive Branch*, the *Underground* would be there as well.

"The bundles are wrapped loose enough," John whispered, "so just find the middle crease in each *Olive Branch* and slide the *Underground* in." He showed them how to push the *Underground* in so it wouldn't fold or stick out.

They began slowly and picked up speed. Lionel and Ryan stuffed as quickly as the older kids did. In a half hour they were almost through the first two stacks.

"How do we keep these from the principal and the *Olive Branch* staff?" Vicki said.

"The short bundle on the end is for the administration and news staff," John said. "Those get delivered to the office and to the teachers' mailboxes. That's the stack we leave alone."

"But if somebody rats on us," Vicki said, "we're back where we started, right?"

"True," Mark said. "But this time I'm betting most will think the school changed their minds. I say they don't find it until second period, and by then the whole school will have them."

Vicki was glad to be at the hospital instead of trying to stay awake in class. The nurse who had admitted Shelly told her, "Your friend is resting, but you can go in."

"What I'd like to do is sleep," Vicki said.

"There's no one else in the room," the nurse said. "Come on."

Shelly slept with her back to the door. The nurse gave Vicki a blanket and pillow and showed her a cushioned chair in the corner.

When she awoke, light streamed into the room and Vicki smelled breakfast. Shelly was sitting up.

"You been here all night?" Shelly said.

"I came early this morning." Vicki slid her chair closer. "How do you feel?"

"Like warmed-up death," Shelly said. "I thought I'd wake up in heaven or—you know."

Vicki wanted to ask the questions that

burned inside her. She didn't want to scare Shelly away, but she was through hedging. There were no friends to distract them, no bell to stop their conversation. Now was the time.

"Why'd you do it, Shel'?"

"It's easy for you," Shelly said. "You got a whole new life."

"I lost my family and my house burned down with everything I own."

"You have people who care about you. You have all that God stuff too. All I have is—well, you saw my mom."

Vicki stood and took Shelly's hand. She looked so hardened, and yet fragile. Like a shell.

"We've known each other since we were kids. We used to be able to say anything. Everything."

Shelly looked away.

"I don't know what pushed you over the edge," Vicki said, "but I don't think you called to say good-bye. I think you hoped I would get there in time to help you. I'm here. I want to know. Nothing you say can stop me from caring. Tell me what's going on."

"I can't," Shelly said. "I don't even want to think about it."

"What does that say about me if you can't even tell me?"

Shelly stiffened. Her brown hair hung

straight. Her eyes were lifeless pools. Vicki decided to be quiet and let her words sink in. She prayed silently and kept holding Shelly's hand. Finally, Shelly turned her weary gaze toward Vicki.

"I was baby-sitting at the Fischers. I had both kids in bed—everything was fine. I wasn't on the phone, didn't have anybody over. I was being good.

"The Fischers were late. Really late. And just when they pulled in the driveway, Maddie started crying. I mean really wailing. So I went to her room, but she wouldn't stop. I picked her up, and then Ben started crying. So I carried them both out—"

Shelly closed her eyes and slumped forward. Telling this story seemed to make Shelly relive it. Every word seemed to hurt.

"Ben was hanging onto my neck, and the baby was still crying, looking right at me. Remember how sweet she was, Vick'?"

"She was a doll."

Shelly stared into the distance. "It's like a dream. I remember every detail like it happened in slow motion. Mr. Fischer was parking the car under the carport, the trailer door opened, Mrs. Fischer saw I had both kids and looked like she felt sorry for me. I was glad she didn't look like she was blaming me for them being awake that late. She started towards me and reached for them as Mr. Fischer came in.

"And then the kids were gone. Both of them. It was like they jumped out of my arms, leaving their diapers and pajamas. I held my arms out and stared, then looked up at the Fischers and they had disappeared right out of their clothes too."

"It must have been awful," Vicki said.

"I didn't know what to do. I just stood there for the longest time."

Vicki could see Shelly still couldn't shake the feelings.

"Why did God have to take those kids, Vicki? They didn't do anything wrong."

"God wasn't punishing anyone, Shel'. He took them to heaven. You don't have to feel bad about that."

Shelly pulled her hand away. "But I do. I'm guilty."

"Why? What did you do?"

"I can't tell you. That's why I wanted to die. I wanted to make sure nobody ever knew."

***

Judd took a school paper from the news bin and tucked it into his backpack. Half the papers were gone now. So far, so good.

Mr. Shellenberger was late to first period

psychology. He apologized and started writing on the board. A tall, fleshy man, as he moved the chalk his hair waved like limp spaghetti. Two students tittered in the corner. Mr. Shellenberger turned, his generous nose in profile.

"Something you'd like to share with the class?" he said.

The room fell silent.

"Come, come. Tell us. I'm sure we'd all like to join in the fun."

One boy shifted nervously.

"It's nothing funny. We just thought we weren't supposed to have this *Underground* thing. Now they've gone and put it in the school paper."

"What are you talking about?" Mr. Shellenberger said. "I saw nothing in my copy of the *Olive Branch.*"

"Well, I've got one right here in the middle of mine," the boy said. He held up the *Underground.* Others opened their papers and found it as well.

"Let me see that," Mr. Shellenberger said.

I have to stall him, Judd thought. *Keep him from reporting this too soon.*

Mr. Shellenberger studied the *Underground* for a moment.

"Why would they change their policy on this?" Judd blurted. Mr. Shellenberger looked at him and shrugged, then turned back to the paper. Judd continued, "I mean, why would the school outlaw this one day and the very next day include it in all our papers? Is there something psychological going on?"

The class laughed.

"You tell me, Thompson. What do you think?"

"Maybe it's guilt," Judd said. "You know, for years we hear how important free speech is and freedom of the press. Maybe they thought it over and let this thing go through because they felt guilty about the double standard."

"Interesting," Mr. Shellenberger said. "Anyone else?"

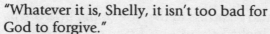

"Whatever it is, Shelly, it isn't too bad for God to forgive."

"You don't know what I've done, Vicki."

Vicki walked to the window. "I know what *I've* done," she said. "It's as bad as anything you could ever dream. I could hardly believe God could forgive me."

"God can't forgive me," Shelly said. "I'd have to spend the rest of my life making up for what I've done."

"That's where you're wrong," Vicki said.

"You can't make up for your sins. You could never do that. Just one is enough to separate you from God."

"Then how are you supposed to make it right?"

Vicki explained that Jesus came to pay the penalty for sin. Because he was perfect, he fulfilled God's demands. His sacrifice allowed anyone who believed he died for them to come back to God.

"It sounds too easy," Shelly said. "You just believe something and it happens."

"Simple but not easy," Vicki said. "It cost a lot. To know what Jesus went through for you—"

"God can't forgive what I've done," Shelly said. "No way it could be that simple."

"You don't understand God. No sin is too great."

Vicki returned to the side of the bed. Shelly still looked stony.

"Is this about the baby?" Vicki said.

"Not the Fischer's baby."

"Then what? You can trust me, Shel', you know that."

"You won't tell anybody?"

"Never."

There was a knock and Shelly's doctor entered. He asked Vicki to step out while he examined Shelly.

"I'll be right back, Shelly," she said.

"Don't you have to get to school?"

"Let me worry about that."

※

Mr. Shellenberger had taken the class on a tour of the history of guilt, including the Puritan concept of good and evil. Whenever he seemed to be winding down, Judd asked another question and he was off again.

A student near Judd asked, "Is this going to be on the test?"

The bell rang before Mr. Shellenberger could answer. Judd saw him take a copy of the *Underground* toward the office. Mark was right. It would be second period before officials discovered what they had distributed themselves.

Judd felt a buzz in his pocket. He pulled out the gizmo John and Mark had given him. The screen read, "Pray for Shelly." He ran into John and Mark in the hall.

"Something's up," John said. "We've just been called to the office. Anybody who worked for the school paper in the last three years has to be there."

"Looks like the *Underground* is toast," Mark said.

"Be careful," Judd said. "Remember, you don't have to volunteer information."

As he headed to his next class, Judd silently prayed that God would keep John and Mark from being found out, and then he prayed for Shelly.

Judd hit the reply button on the tiny machine. "Pray for John and Mark," he tapped in. "*Underground* discovered."

"She's been through a lot," the doctor told Vicki as he left Shelly's room. "I wouldn't push her emotionally."

"I just want to be her friend."

"Maybe the best thing is to let her rest."

"But—"

"Tell her you have to get to school," the doctor said. "You can come back this afternoon when she's had a chance to rest."

Vicki tried again but the doctor made sense. "If you care for your friend, you'll come back later."

Vicki hated leaving Shelly now, when Shelly needed her most. She entered the room to find Shelly watching TV.

"The doc says I ought to let you rest awhile," Vicki said.

"Yeah, thanks for coming."

"I'll stay if you want."

"We can talk later," Shelly said.

So close, Vicki thought, thankful for the opportunity but disappointed at the delay. *So close*.

SEVEN

Breakthrough

VICKI was surprised to find the school office crowded with students. She pushed her way to the secretary's desk to report in and noticed John and Mark in the conference room. John nodded and Vicki took the hint. She sat unnoticed in the outer office where she could hear what was going on.

Coach Handlesman and Principal Jenness were talking to the English teacher, Mr. Carlson, adviser to the school newspaper. Handlesman fumed, "We had people on both sides of the school. No way anyone could have gotten to the papers without being spotted."

"This was an inside job," Mrs. Jenness said. "Someone here did this or knows who did."

"Somebody had to get to these papers before they arrived," Handlesman said. "I want to know which of you picked the papers up from the printer this morning?"

"That would be me," Mr. Carlson said sheepishly. "I brought them in my van and some kids helped me put them in the bins. I was with them the whole time."

"How many of you kids have ever been to the print plant?" Handlesman said. "So unless someone's lying, seven of you have knowledge of when and where the papers are picked up."

Vicki assumed John and Mark raised their hands. Mr. Carlson would have been alarmed if they hadn't. She slipped into the hallway as Coach Handlesman barked something about expelling all the journalism students unless the culprits confessed. The heat was being turned up on Nicolae Carpathia High School.

At lunch she met in the cafeteria with Judd and John and Mark. The cousins were still shaken.

Mark said, "Nobody admitted anything, and I thought Jenness was going to expel us all."

"That's when the fire alarm rang," John said. "Talk about timing."

"You'd think they would have postponed the drill when they had a big meeting going," Judd said.

"It wasn't exactly a scheduled drill," Vicki said. "Somebody hit a fire alarm."

"How do you know?" Judd said.

Vicki smiled.

"No," Judd said.

"Vicki to the rescue!" Mark said, and gave her a high five.

"That sure settled things," John said. "When the fire department gets called for nothing, the principal's not too happy. After everybody got back inside, I think they were more interested in confiscating the *Underground* than finding out who actually put the thing together."

"One of the reporters told me the office collected a few hundred copies," Mark said. "That means there're still a thousand or more out there."

"Why is this such a big deal to Handlesman?" John said. "He's the guy who took our Bibles too."

"Good question," Judd said. "What does he have to gain or lose by a couple of Bibles or the *Underground*?"

"About those Bibles," Mark said. "Last week they turned up in our lockers."

"You're kidding," Vicki said. "Are you sure they're the same ones?"

"Yeah, they have our names in them and some of the verses are highlighted."

"It's the weirdest thing," John said. "No note, no explanation. I can't figure who would have access to them."

"We'd better cool it a couple of days," Judd said. "Let's not press our luck. We'll see you two guys in a few days."

That night at home Judd filled in Lionel and Ryan, and everybody agreed it had been an amazing day. Then Bruce called.

"I need to see the four of you right away," he said.

"Something wrong?" Judd said. "We wanted to go with Vicki to—"

"I'll tell you when you get here. Come as quickly as you can."

Bruce was alone at his desk. Judd told him Vicki needed to get back to her friend at the hospital soon. "This won't take long," Bruce said. To Judd, Bruce looked as grave as he had ever seen him. "Sit down."

Bruce moved to the front of his desk and sat on the edge. "I am very concerned about what's going on at your school."

Bruce waited as if to see if anyone would explain. "I'm talking about the newspaper," he said. "I admire your desire, but I disagree with the way you've done this."

"How did you find out?" Judd said.

"Buck told me about Vicki's call and I put two and two together. But I never dreamed you were thinking about something for the whole school. You didn't seek my advice. You put each other in danger. And you've evidently gotten two other boys involved as well."

Judd exploded, "I can't believe this! Yes, we took some chances, and no, we didn't ask you to hold our hands. Sure we could have been caught, but we thought it was worth the risk."

Bruce looked stunned. Judd felt Vicki's hand on his arm, but he pulled away.

"You keep saying we don't know how much time we have left, that people need Jesus before it's too late. So we do something about it and you criticize us for taking risks!"

"Now, Judd—"

"I know you're our pastor, but you're not our father. I don't know what everybody else thinks, but I'm prepared to risk this and a lot more. If it means the difference between people going to heaven or hell, I don't care what happens to me."

Judd didn't realize he had risen from his chair. He looked around, embarrassed at the shocked looks. Judd sat and took a deep breath. "Bruce, you didn't even ask who Vicki was going to see in the hospital. Part of the reason Vicki even has a chance to talk with Shelly is the *Underground*."

"It's not like we didn't think this through," Vicki said. "It's hard to be criticized when so far only good has come from it."

"I'm proud of you," Bruce said, "and I know you have the right motives, but—" He sighed and ran a hand through his hair. "I don't know how much I can tell you."

"About what?" Lionel said.

Bruce pulled a copy of the *Underground* from his desk. "There is another underground believer at Nicolae High. This person believes you're all in grave danger."

"A Christian teacher?" Vicki said.

"I didn't say that," Bruce said. "I was asked not to reveal this person's identity, and I expect you to respect that."

"They know who we are?" Vicki said.

"Process of elimination," Bruce said. "This person heard about you through me. Assumptions about your identity were made when the *Underground* showed up."

"How do they, or you, know about the other two guys?"

"Their Bibles were confiscated and they worked for the school paper last year. They were in some meeting today?"

Judd nodded. "If whoever this is is worried

about us being expelled, that's not exactly grave danger."

"Expulsion would endanger the whole group and your setup," Bruce said. "But this is worse than expulsion. Because of the high profile of the school, Global Community forces want to make this a test case. They're talking about assigning GC monitors to the school, people with the authority to make arrests."

"Why would they be worried about us?" Ryan said. "We're just a bunch of kids."

"But you're talking about things Carpathia can't tolerate. The Antichrist and his henchmen won't allow proselytizing in a school named after him."

"What's pros—"

"Proselytizing," Lionel said. "Trying to get people to believe what you believe."

"Pretty soon it'll be illegal," Bruce said.

"To even talk to people about it?" Ryan said.

"That's right."

"You think they'll start taking *all* the Bibles away?"

"That wouldn't surprise me."

Ryan shook his head. "So why don't we gather up all the Bibles we can and hide them? Later on we can give them to the people who want to read them."

"Not a bad idea," Bruce said. "Where would you hide them?"

"Not here," Ryan said, "because that's the first place they'd look. We could stash them in Judd's garage or in his basement until we find a better place."

"First we'd have to find a bunch of Bibles," Judd said.

"That's easy," Ryan said. "The people who disappeared had lots of 'em. I found some in a house the other day that looked like they'd never been used. I think the looters took everything else."

"Looks like you guys have at least one new mission," Bruce said, and Judd could tell it meant a lot to Ryan that he had come up with a plan of his own.

"Before you go," Bruce said, "tell me a little about Vicki's friend. I'm sorry I didn't ask earlier."

After Vicki told him of her conversation with Shelly, Bruce prayed for her. "And you know what, kids?" he said. "I need you to be praying for me too. As I think about the pull I feel to travel and trying to unite the little pockets of what the Bible calls the 'tribulation saints,' I don't know how I'm going to do it."

"We'll pray for you," Judd said. "And I'm sorry for blowing up like that."

"I forgive you. Like the rest of us, your strength is your weakness. You know what that means?"

Judd shook his head. "The same passion you have for God also gives you a short fuse. On one side it's a strength. On the other, it's a weakness. Something to work on."

⁕

When Vicki walked into Shelly's hospital room, Shelly's mother was by the bed. She rambled about her problems while she flipped through television channels looking for who-knew-what. She acted as if Shelly was just sick and seemed oblivious to the fact that Shelly had tried to take her own life.

"I need to grab a bite to eat," she said just before visiting hours were over. "I'll be back to say goodnight."

Shelly shook her head as her mother left. "She needs a drink. That's what she's leaving for."

Vicki couldn't wait any longer. "I promised I would keep your secret, Shelly. Whatever it is, God can forgive you. You mentioned something about a baby before I had to go?"

Shelly pulled at her fingers and looked toward the door.

"We're alone now—you don't have to worry," Vicki said.

"I never told anybody about this," Shelly said. "It's about Mom. I went with her to the doctor because she was feeling funny, and the tests came back positive. She was pregnant."

"I don't understand," Vicki said. "Why would you feel guilty for your mother being pregnant?"

"I hated her so much, Vick.' I couldn't stand living there anymore. She told me not to, but I told Dad. She said he'd move out, that he'd leave us alone, but I was so mad at her. They yelled and screamed the whole night, and the next day he was gone. It's my fault, Vick'."

"You know that's not true, Shel'," Vicki said. "People make their own decisions. Your dad would've found out anyway, right?"

"Not if she'd had an abortion."

Shelly looked like she was about to cry.

"To be honest, I was kinda excited to have a little brother or sister. I thought maybe I could take care of it, that it would make things better. I thought Mom might get some help, might sober up. But that night, when the Fischers and their babies vanished, God took my mom's baby too. He punished me for what I did."

Shelly collapsed into tears and Vicki embraced her. Shelly's mother did not return, so Vicki called Judd and told him she was staying the night. She was there, dozing in the chair, when Shelly awoke in the morning.

EIGHT

A Friend for Ryan

"WE'VE all done bad things, Shel'," Vicki said as they ate breakfast together in Shelly's hospital room.

"You really think God could forgive me?"

"I know it's hard to believe, but that's what he promises. He can make you a new person."

Shelly hesitated. "Like I said, it sounds too good to be true."

"It's a gift, Shel'. We all missed it the first time around. That's why we're still here."

"But if you've hated somebody all your life, and you've split your mom and dad apart just to be mean, it doesn't seem right."

"God can forgive any sin, Shel', trust me. It's not how much we've sinned that's important—it's how much God loves us."

"What do you do to make this all happen?" Shelly said. "Do I have to kneel or something?"

"I didn't," Vicki said. "I don't think God cares, as long as your heart is in the right position. Know what I mean?"

"Yeah. I guess I want to do it, but I don't know what to say."

"You want to pray after me?"

"You mean say what you say?"

"Sure. If you mean it, God will know."

Shelly nodded and closed her eyes. She repeated each phrase after Vicki. "Dear God, I know I'm a sinner. Please forgive me. Thank you for dying on the cross for my sins so I wouldn't have to pay the penalty myself. Please come into my life and make me a new person. And thank you for promising that I will go to heaven to be with you when I die. In Jesus' name, amen."

"That's it?" Shelly said. "I don't feel any different. Don't I have to do something else?"

"The only thing you need to do now is follow him."

Vicki was thrilled later to be able to tell Judd on the way to school, "We finally have another female member of the Young Tribulation Force!"

A line of kids stretched in front of the school when Judd and Vicki arrived. Judd strained to see what was going on and finally tapped a boy on the shoulder and asked.

"They're searching everybody," he said, "I think because of that underground paper."

Judd and Vicki finally made it through the doors and found the assistant principal and a Global Community guard going through backpacks. They were searching every third student.

"You," the Global Community worker said to Judd, "over here."

Vicki was waved on. She stopped at her locker and looked back. A commotion arose. Shouting. Books flying.

"That's not mine!" someone shouted. "Let me go!"

A Global Community worker led a student away. Judd slipped out of line unnoticed and joined Vicki.

"I think they found some booze in his backpack," Judd said.

"This is just what Bruce was afraid of. How are we going to get copies through now?"

During announcements, Principal Jenness described the searches as "unfortunately necessary. We're sorry many were inconvenienced this morning. If we knew who the perpetrators were, we wouldn't have to con-

duct such searches. Any helpful information
will be rewarded."

That night when the kids met with Bruce,
Vicki loved seeing his reaction when he
heard about Shelly.

Judd said, "It makes me want to do
another edition of the *Underground* soon."

"I can imagine," Bruce said. "I wanted you
to play it safe, but now I don't know what to
say. There's more danger than ever—I know
that. Let me show you what you're up
against." He turned a television monitor and
pushed Play on the VCR.

A Global Community CNN reporter
explained how President Gerald Fitzhugh
had called upon nations of the world to
study Nicolae Carpathia's proposal to do
away with all weapons. As a goodwill gesture, the President gave a new 757 airplane
to the United Nations. It would be named
"Global Community One."

Carpathia gazed directly into the camera,
appearing to look right into the eyes of each
viewer. His voice was quiet and emotional.

"I would like to thank President Fitzhugh
for this most generous gesture. We at the
United Nations are deeply moved, grateful,

and humbled. We look forward to a wonderful ceremony in Jerusalem next Monday."

Bruce turned off the TV. "We need to pray for Rayford Steele," he said. "You know he and his daughter Chloe go to this church. We believe he will be asked to fly that plane for Carpathia."

"He'd be in almost as much danger as Judd and Vicki, wouldn't he?" Ryan joked.

"What ceremony is Carpathia talking about?" Vicki said.

"I believe it's the signing of a treaty between Israel and the new one-world government. If it is, it will signal the beginning of the seven-year Tribulation I've told you about. There are other signs. All nations are to convert their money to dollars within the year, so we'll have a one-world currency. It's almost too much to believe. There's also talk of a one-world religion, which was also prophesied in Scripture.

"Pieces of the one-world government are falling into place more quickly than I ever thought possible."

Vicki and Bruce visited Shelly at her trailer the next evening. Shelly looked pale, but there was a smile Vicki hadn't seen for ages. Shelly seemed nervous around Bruce at first, but Vicki assured her he was there only to help her understand more about the Bible.

Bruce stood when Shelly's mom walked into the room. Her hair was a mess and she smelled of alcohol. Shelly said, "You know Vicki, Mom. This is her friend, Pastor Barnes."

"A pastor? What are you doing here?"

"Just talking to Shelly about God," Bruce said. "Feel free to join us." Shelly's mother squinted warily at him but sat next to her daughter on the couch as Bruce pulled up a chair. First he told his own story, about how he'd been a phony for so many years and then lost his wife and children when he was left behind at the Rapture. He said he had finally prayed and received Christ into his life.

"Shelly made that same decision last night," Bruce said.

"I don't believe in religion," Shelly's mom said.

"This is not religion," Bruce said. "Religion is our way of trying to reach God. This is a relationship with a personal God who wants to help us."

"I don't need help."

Bruce didn't argue. He just pointed out specific Scriptures and explained them. Vicki knew he wanted Shelly to be sure she was going to heaven some day.

"In 1 John 1:9 we are told that if we confess our sins, God is faithful to forgive our sins and cleanse us from unrighteousness. And near the end of the Gospel of John, the writer says, 'These things are written that you may believe that Jesus is the Christ, the Son of God, and that by believing you may have life in His name.' The book of Romans says that everyone who calls upon the name of the Lord will be saved."

"The people who disappeared were the saved ones, Mom," Shelly said.

"That's right," Bruce said. "Just like you now, Shelly."

Shelly's mom struggled to push herself up off the couch. She looked down on Bruce. "Get out of my house," she said. "You're try-ing to brainwash my girl."

"Mom! Just listen!"

"I won't," she said. "Now get out!"

※

The next day a still-dejected Vicki walked with Ryan as he darted in and out of various neighborhoods. Though she thought it unnecessary, she carried a huge trash bag. Ryan believed he could find enough Bibles to fill it, and Vicki didn't argue. He was so excited about this adventure that she didn't want to stifle him.

Ryan would find an abandoned house and walk right in. "I found seven in here!" he would call to Vicki. He plunked them into the bottom of the bag and ran off again. *He was right,* Vicki thought. *I'll never be able to drag this home.*

They came to the brick shell of a burned-out house.

"Stay out of there," Vicki said. "It's too dangerous. Anyway, everything's burned!"

"Something's in there," Ryan shouted, running ahead. He pushed aside the charred remains of the front door and a sooty beam came crashing down, just missing him.

"Get out, Ryan!" Vicki said as she ran to the house.

"Wait!" he said. "There's somebody or something in here!"

Vicki followed him in and saw something moving in the rubble. Ryan got close and it whimpered. Black as coal, it looked like a wild animal. Ryan knelt and held out his hand, and the animal sniffed. Finally, it gingerly moved toward him. Vicki held her breath as Ryan gathered it in his arms.

"What is it?" Vicki said.

"Our new dog," Ryan said. "He looks like he hasn't eaten in weeks."

Ryan was as dirty as the pup, but it occurred to Vicki that this was the answer to her prayers. She had prayed that God would take some of the pain from him. Maybe this new companion would do just that.

"No way," Judd said. "He's not bringing that filthy thing into my house. It looks more like a rat than a dog."

Ryan handed the dog to Vicki and ran inside, returning with a piece of hot dog. "Come here, boy!"

The dog lunged at the food and nearly nipped Ryan's finger.

"Just like a rat," Judd said.

"Can I talk with you, Judd?" Vicki said. "In private?"

Vicki and Judd went into the den. Judd had begun the next edition of the *Underground* and the place was cluttered.

"You have to understand what this means to Ryan," she said. "What could it hurt?"

Judd shook his head. "It's not practical. We're trying to do some radical things here that take up most of our time. What happens when the dog doesn't get fed or isn't let out, and Ryan's not around?"

"Make it his responsibility. It'll be good for him. For all of us."

She was right and Judd knew it. She was in tune with Ryan in a way he could never be.

"Don't blame me if it doesn't work," he

said. "The first time Ryan messes up, the dog goes."

Vicki was elated to see the change in Ryan. He went straight to work giving it a bath. Judd had invited John and Mark over to work on the next *Underground*. Everybody seemed stunned when Ryan unwrapped the dog and revealed its white fur.

"What's his name?" Mark said.

"Call him Rapture," Lionel said.

"How about Ashes?" Vicki said.

"Wait," Ryan said. "What was that bird that came out of the ashes?"

"The Phoenix," John said.

"That's it! I'll name him Phoenix."

Judd told John he wanted the next edition of the *Underground* to cover the Israel treaty. "We'll deliver it Friday and the treaty will be signed Monday. That ought to convince people we're onto something."

"How are you gonna do it," Lionel said, "with all those Global Community thugs around?"

"They aren't going to be there every day," John said. He pulled out of his pocket what looked like a tiny radio. "We put a transmitter on Mrs. Jenness's desk. It's a tiny smiley face at the end of her stapler. This receiver has to be within a hundred yards, and sometimes it doesn't work too well, but we heard her say the Global Community guys would be back Friday. That's when the *Olive Branch* gets distributed again. We can't risk that scheme again."

"I can think of only one way to get the paper to everyone," Vicki said. "And we'll have to use Ryan to do it "

"Me?" Ryan said.

"Yeah," Vicki said. "Are you willing?"

"I am," Lionel said. "I don't care what happens to me anymore."

"Me neither," Ryan said.

"*Either*," Lionel said.

NINE

Fugitives

LATE Thursday night, Judd drove Vicki, Lionel, and Ryan to Nicolae High, where Vicki had left a window slightly open, leading to the showers in the gym locker room.

Judd parked a few blocks away and each kid grabbed a box filled with the *Underground*.

This was their best issue yet. With John's expertise with the publishing program, it looked professionally printed. Readers of the *Underground* would learn that the Bible predicted the signing of the treaty that coming Monday. Assuming it came off as the paper outlined, readers should be convinced that the writers knew what they were talking about. They would be urged to give their lives to Christ before the beginning of the Tribulation. John and Mark had even included an untraceable E-mail address where students could write for more information and a Bible study.

The kids knew the prophecy could also backfire. If Bruce was wrong about the signing of the peace treaty with Israel, their message wouldn't ring true. It was a risk they were willing to take.

All four wore dark clothing. Each carried a winter hat that pulled over their faces. They had heard rumors of surveillance cameras.

Judd and Lionel were to creep to the rear entrance of the school where it would be easy to hide behind the evergreens. Vicki and Ryan crawled along the rear wall to an inner courtyard. The place was well lit, so when Vicki gave the signal, they dashed to the other side, Ryan following her into the darkness.

They gingerly made their way down a few steps to what smelled like a cellar. A dim bulb above lit a huge door with bars across the window. A little farther down was a small, cobweb-filled window. "This is the one I left slightly open," Vicki said. "We're right under the gym near the showers."

Vicki pushed and the window gave way. "Can you squeeze through?"

"It's tight," Ryan said. "No wonder you didn't want to do this. Looks like the spiders are having a party."

"Yuck! Go left to the stairwell and up to the gym, across the basketball court to the back entrance. Those are the only doors I could find that don't have alarms."

Vicki returned to Judd and Lionel. They wouldn't approach the school until Ryan opened the door.

"What's taking him so long?" Lionel whispered.

"It's a long way," Vicki said. "And pretty dark. He probably has to feel his way along."

"What if a janitor or night watchman is in there?" Judd said. "Or one of the Global Community guys?"

"Don't even think about it," Vicki said.

The wind picked up. Judd and Lionel sat on the open boxes to keep the papers from flying and pulled their hats down over their faces.

"Look," Vicki said. A door opened at the end of the gym. Ryan stuck out his hand with his thumb up.

The three raced to the gym, boxes in tow. In seconds they were safely inside.

"I took a wrong turn and wound up in a big storage room," Ryan said. "It's like a dungeon. Perfect place to store my Bibles. I had to wait under the stairs when a janitor came down. He's sweeping or dusting or something in the locker room."

"Then we've got to hurry," Judd said. "And be ready to hide if you hear him."

"You'll hear him," Ryan said. "He's carrying a big ring of jangly keys."

They split into two pairs, Judd and Ryan taking one end of the school, Vicki and Lionel the other. They would meet in the middle. They folded copies of the *Underground* and slid one through the vent opening in each locker. It was slow work. It was 2 A.M. when they finally met near the front office.

"Look up there in the grate," Judd said. "They did install cameras. They'll be checking the tape tomorrow."

"Can we go now?" Ryan said. "I want to check on Phoenix and make sure he's OK."

"Ryan, wait!" Vicki said. Before she could stop him, Ryan pushed open the fire doors at the front of the school. A shrill alarm filled the hallway. Ryan turned, wide-eyed. "I didn't mean to," he mouthed.

"This way!" Judd shouted, and they raced back to the gym. When they reached the back doors, Vicki heard the janitor's keys bouncing. He was closing in. Judd quickly opened the doors and started out, but stopped. A siren. Tires on gravel.

"We can make it," Lionel said.

"We have a better chance hiding," Judd

said. "It's an open field. They'll see us out there for sure."

"The dungeon," Ryan said.

And they bolted downstairs in the darkness, putting distance between themselves and the jangling keys.

Vicki could feel the spiders. Everywhere. She shuddered and stayed close to Judd. After a few minutes their eyes adjusted to the dark. They were in an inner chamber underneath the gymnasium. Boxes of paper and school supplies were stacked around the room. The four huddled behind water-stained boxes.

"Don't worry," Ryan whispered as he swiped at the cobwebs. "These are only spider leftovers. They won't hurt you."

Judd fiddled with something in his pocket, then raised his hand for quiet. They heard footsteps overhead.

"They're in the gym," Lionel said. "I hope they don't have dogs."

"Dogs?" Vicki said.

The footsteps came closer. A beam of light waved through the hallway. A man shouted and another joined him.

"Here's the window they came through," one man said. "I heard 'em. I was workin' down the hall there. They probably came in to spray paint a few walls. I'll bet we scared 'em and they took off the same way they came in."

A light shone near the dungeon.

"Stinks down here," the first man said.

"Tell me about it. I'm here almost every night and I'm still not used to it. Let's get out of here."

The kids waited a few minutes, then tip-toed to the gym. The men were gone. Judd opened the back doors of the gym and motioned the others toward the car.

As the back door closed, a light flashed in their faces. Colored lights. A voice on a loud-speaker. "Police! Stop right there!"

"Scatter!" Judd yelled. "Try to get back to the car!"

Vicki ran with Ryan. The police car threw gravel and went another direction. Toward Judd, she thought. She and Ryan ran past the football field toward town. When they came near houses they stopped to catch their breath.

"Where's the car?" Ryan said.

"That way," Vicki said, gasping. "You run pretty fast."

Vicki and Ryan took the long route and made their way across lawns and through alleys. A dog startled Vicki when it snapped at them through a chain link fence. When they finally made it back to the car, neither Judd nor Lionel was in sight.

A car approached with its headlights off, so Vicki and Ryan crouched beside Judd's car.

"They're not there," a voice said.

"That's Judd," Ryan said, standing.

"Don't!" Vicki said, but it was too late.

"Hey," Judd said. "You made it."

"How did you?" Vicki said, standing. Judd and Lionel were in the backseat, John and Mark in the front.

"I got Judd's SOS on the gizmo," John said, "and we got here just in time to see these two running for their lives."

Judd found sleep impossible. He wandered down to the living room and found the others so keyed up that they were sitting around the living room talking. "We're all running on empty," he said. "Too many short nights in a row. Even if we can't sleep, we need to get to bed and at least rest. Tomorrow Nicolae High is going to get its strongest dose yet of the *Underground*.

Judd finally fell asleep just before dawn and made everybody late for school. As he and Vicki hurried in, she said, "I thought the GC guys would be searching everybody again."

Judd shrugged. "Me too," he said, just as

they came upon hundreds of students lined up in the hallway. School administrators and Global Community monitors went from locker to locker with garbage bags searching for copies of the *Underground.* Mr. Handlesman barked at kids and banged on their lockers if they were too slow.

"Students with lockers in the east hallway only, report there immediately," Mrs. Jenness said over the loudspeaker. "Everyone else, remain in your class."

John rushed up to Judd and Vicki. "Everybody who went to their lockers before first period got one," John whispered. "Now the office is in damage-control mode. You should hear students, though, Judd. Everybody's talking about it."

Vicki's gym class sat in the bleachers, still dressed. Mrs. Waltonen conferred with an assistant as the girls sat and talked. Vicki sat near the front and listened.

"Why don't they want us to read this stuff?" one girl said.

"It's dangerous," another said.

"It says there's going to be some treaty signed Monday. It's supposed to be predicted in the Bible."

"I never understood the Bible."

"This says you can, though. It makes sense to me."

All around Vicki girls were whispering, "I want to read it. I don't care what they say. If I find one, I'm keeping it." She was ecstatic. This was just what the Trib Force had been hoping for.

At the end of the period, Mr. Handlesman's voice came over the loudspeaker.

"We've just witnessed the last incident of rebellion at Nicolae Carpathia High School. We *will* find those responsible, and we will find them *today*. Anyone with any information that can help us should report to the office now."

Kids walked through the halls carefully, as if through a war zone. Vicki knew better but felt people looked at her strangely, like they knew of her involvement.

In Vicki's English class, Mr. Carlson asked, "How many have actually read this underground paper?"

A few raised their hands. Vicki knew there had to be more but couldn't tell if they were afraid or really hadn't looked at the *Underground*.

"Why do you think this publication is so threatening to those in charge here?" Mr. Carlson said.

"There are a lot of kooks out there," a girl

said. Vicki knew she was on the staff of the *Olive Branch*. "Maybe they're trying to manipulate us by scaring us about Mr. Carpathia being the Antichrist."

"Kooks is right," someone else said. "I thought all those people were gone."

"And what if one of those kooks is one of you?" Carlson said. "A schoolmate? A classmate?"

Kids looked around the room, laughing and pointing at each other. Vicki felt her cheeks flush. Mr. Carlson tried to restore order, but he was unsuccessful until Coach Handlesman entered with two Global Community guards. The room got deathly quiet. The guards stood by the door as Handlesman spoke to Mr. Carlson.

"You have to be kidding," Carlson said with a laugh. "There must be a mistake."

Coach Handlesman turned to the class. "Which one of you is Vicki Byrne?"

Vicki held her breath as everyone turned and looked at her.

"Come with us, Miss Byrne," the coach said.

"Why?" she said. "What?"

Coach Handlesman approached her desk. He leaned inches from her face.

"We know," he said. "It's over."

TEN

Betrayed

BETWEEN classes Mark found Judd and pulled him into an audiovisual department closet down the hall from the front office. John had hooked a small speaker to the receiver. "I got a message from Vicki that she had been found out," he said.

Judd looked at his own message receiver. It was off. "Oh no."

"She's not in the office yet," John said, his ear near the speaker. "At least I haven't heard anybody yet."

"My battery must be dead," Judd said. "Tell Lionel and Ryan to pray for Vicki." Mark punched in the message. "And just in case, add a line to tell Vicki we're with her."

"Wait, I hear something," John said. "Somebody just came in and sat down." They all huddled closer. Judd heard crying and hoped that wasn't Vicki. He knew she was tougher than that.

A woman's voice cut through the static. "Stop blubbering. Tell them what you know and get the money."

"Nobody said the reward was money, Mom," a girl said. "Why are you making me do this?"

"It'll be money, all right. Tell them everything. I want to get out of here too. I got places to go."

Judd felt helpless. He wished he had been caught. Instead, Vicki was about to take the blame for them all.

"How did they find Vicki?" Mark said.

"Somebody must have turned her in," Judd said.

Two GC guards sat behind Vicki and in front of the closed door to Principal Jenness's inner office. Vicki felt a vibration and peeked at the tiny screen in her pocket.

"Pray for Vicki—Caught," it read. Then, "If you see this, hang in, Vick'."

She prayed silently, "Please give me the right words. And thank you for my friends."

Coach Handlesman and Mrs. Jenness entered. He pulled a chair near her, letting it scrape across the floor. Mrs. Jenness leaned against a file cabinet, arms folded. The two adults stared at her for what seemed an eternity.

"Why'd you do it?" Handlesman said.

"What did I do?"

"You know what you did," Mrs. Jenness said. "Why did you trip the alarm the other day?"

Vicki stared at her.

"C'mon, Byrne," Handlesman said. "We saw it on tape, and we also compared the video of the kids who broke into the school last night. It was you, Vicki. There's no use trying to hide it any longer. Tell us about it."

She knew they couldn't have seen her face the night before. They were trying to scare her into confessing.

Mrs. Jenness moved to a desk near Vicki and sat. She smiled and tried to sound reassuring.

"You're just misguided," she said. "We don't want to punish you. We just want to find out who's behind this."

Right, Vicki thought. *It had to be somebody else. A girl like me wouldn't have the brains to put two sentences together.*

"Just tell us who put you up to this," Mrs. Jenness said, "and this all goes away."

"Otherwise," Handlesman said, "you go with these guys. Believe me, you don't want to do that."

Vicki turned. The guards stared at her with

blank faces. She cleared her throat. Her voice came out shaky. Scared.

"I'm sorry about the alarm," Vicki said. "I didn't know the fire department would come. Nobody put me up to that. I'll pay a fine or whatever."

"We can overlook a prank like that," Mrs. Jenness said. "But this newspaper—that's much more serious. Why don't you tell us about it, Vicki?"

Vicki remained silent, staring at Handlesman. The coach smiled and looked at the principal.

"She knows," he said. "She knows we couldn't see her face on the video from last night." He turned back to Vicki. "But I wonder if we sent someone to your home in—he looked at a clipboard—Kings Trailer Court. Bet we'd find a mask, huh? Or maybe evidence of your part in producing the *Underground?*"

"We've gotta get her out of there," Judd said.

"We don't know what's going on," John said. "All I can hear is this girl whimpering and her mother."

"How could we get her out?" Mark said. "They've got her. Maybe it's time we faced the music and turned ourselves in."

"That's crazy," John said.

"As crazy as letting her take the fall for all of us?" Mark said. "She saved us the other day with that fire alarm. And for that she gets punished?"

The speaker crackled. Coach Handlesman was in Jenness's office, talking to the woman and the girl. He was asking about Vicki.

"It was her," the woman interrupted. "It had to be."

"She never told me that," the girl said.

"Why do you *think* it was her?" Handlesman said. "Did she mention the newspaper?"

"I brought it up," the girl said. "We talked about stuff in the paper," the girl said. "But she never actually said she was a part of it."

"You've got the guilty one," the woman said. "Can we have the money now?"

"That doesn't prove anything," Handlesman said. "No proof, no reward."

Judd said, "Mark, give me your gadget, quick."

Vicki felt another vibration and reached in her pocket as if peeking at her watch. It read, "Admit nothing. No proof."

How would anyone know that? she wondered, then remembered the bug in Jenness's office behind her.

"You don't need to worry about what time it is, young lady," Mrs. Jenness said. "You'd better be thinking about your future. Things could be pretty grim."

Coach Handlesman returned from Jenness's office, but Vicki couldn't turn around quickly enough to see who was in there before the door closed.

Coach Handlesman pulled up his chair again. "We know this wasn't your idea," he said. "You just got caught up in it. Somebody probably convinced you this would be a noble cause. We can understand that. If you cooperate now, tell us who's involved, we'll see things get worked out for you."

"And if I don't?"

Mrs. Jenness said, "You could be removed from your home and sentenced to a juvenile facility."

"For a fire-alarm prank?" Vicki said.

Handlesman slammed his fist on the table. "We don't care about that!" he screamed. "Tell us about the newspaper!"

"What makes you think it was me?"

Handlesman rose and stood in front of Mrs. Jenness's office. "Here's why," he said.

He opened the door and let it swing wide. Vicki gasped.

Shelly. And her mother. The woman pointed at Vicki.

"That's her," she said. "She's the one with all the crazy ideas. She came over to our house with that pastor of hers. Trying to brainwash my kid."

Shelly didn't speak. She just cried and mouthed, "I'm sorry. I'm so sorry."

Handlesman shut the door. "This is it," he said. "Either tell us the truth or face the consequences."

"I can't take it any more," Mark said. "I'm going in there and tell them it was me."

"Don't," John said. "Let this play out. Maybe you ought to call your pastor, Judd."

"I don't want to get him involved," Judd said. "He said something like this might happen."

"Hey, call him and tell him," John said. "At least he can pray for her."

"You guys really get me," Mark said, and he was out the door and down the hall before John or Judd could stop him.

Vicki was startled by a sharp knock on the office door. Coach Handlesman opened it and Mrs. Waltonen said, "May I see you and Mrs. Jenness a moment? Outside?"

"We're in the middle of something," Mrs. Jenness said.

"I think it will be worth your while," Mrs. Waltonen said.

Handlesman and Jenness left the door

slightly open, and Vicki saw Mark in the hall. She furrowed her brow and mouthed, "What are you doing?"

Mark shrugged. Handlesman said, "Unless you have business here, pal, get lost."

Mark caught Vicki's eye again and put his hand in his pocket, then scurried off. Vicki read his message: "I'll confess."

She quickly tapped back: "NO!"

"If Mark gives it up, we all have to," John said.

"She doesn't want him to," Judd said, looking at John's screen over his shoulder. "Let's keep our heads."

"If Vicki gets out of there without talking, the GC guys will be all over her to see who she hangs with."

Mark came back in. "That's one brave girl. Waltonen is talking to Jenness and Handlesman."

"What about?"

"She said she knows where Vicki hangs out. Waltonen gave them the street you live on, but she couldn't remember the address."

"I knew that would come back to haunt us," Judd said. "Handlesman will be sniffing around the neighborhood all afternoon. How did Vicki look?"

"Like she was on trial."

Vicki sat up as Mrs. Jenness and Coach Handlesman returned. Neither looked at her.

"Anything you want to say?" the coach said finally.

"I'm sorry about the alarm. I won't do it again."

He nodded to the principal.

"We're going to let you think about it overnight, Vicki," she said. "Your future depends on what you tell us. Tomorrow we want you back here with your parents."

Vicki wondered if her mom and dad would be proud of what she was doing. Could they see her? That thought overwhelmed her and she began to cry.

"It's OK, Vicki," Mrs. Jenness said, handing her a tissue. "You have a talk with your family. I'm sure they'll want you to do the right thing."

The bell rang and Coach Handlesman said, "You'd better get to your next class."

Vicki walked out into the stream of students. At the end of the hall Judd, John, and Mark turned and walked the other way. Would they desert her? Did they think she had betrayed them the way Shelly had betrayed her?

For the first time since she had met her new friends, she felt utterly alone.

ABOUT THE AUTHORS

Jerry B. Jenkins (www.jerryjenkins.com) is the writer of the Left Behind series. He is author of more than one hundred books, of which four have reached the *New York Times* best-seller list. Former vice president for publishing for the Moody Bible Institute of Chicago, he also served many years as editor of *Moody* magazine and is now Moody's writer-at-large.

His writing has appeared in publications as varied as *Reader's Digest, Parade,* in-flight magazines, and many Christian periodicals. He has written books in four genres: biography, marriage and family, fiction for children, and fiction for adults.

Jenkins's biographies include books with Hank Aaron, Bill Gaither, Luis Palau, Walter Payton, Orel Hershiser, Nolan Ryan, Brett Butler, and Billy Graham, among many others.

Five of his apocalyptic novel—*Left Behind, Tribulation Force, Nicolae, Soul Harvest,* and *Apollyon*—have appeared on the Christian Booksellers Association's best-selling fiction list and the *Publishers Weekly* religion best-sellers list. *Left Behind* was nominated for Novel of the Year by the Evangelical Christian Publishers Association in both 1997 and 1998.

As a marriage and family author and speaker, Jenkins has been a frequent guest on Dr. James Dobson's *Focus on the Family* radio program.

Jerry is also the writer of the nationally syndicated sports story comic strip *Gil Thorp,* distributed to newspapers across the United States by Tribune Media Services.

Jerry and his wife, Dianna live in Colorado.

Limited speaking engagement information available through speaking@jerryjenkins.com.

Dr. Tim LaHaye (www.timlahaye.org), who conceived the idea of fictionalizing an account of the Rapture and the Tribulation, is a noted author, minister, educator, and nationally recognized speaker on Bible prophecy. He presides over Tim Lahaye Ministries and is chairman and founder of the Pre-Trib Research Center. Presently Dr. LaHaye speaks at many of the major Bible prophecy conferences in the U.S. and Canada, where his seven current prophecy books are very popular.

Dr. LaHaye is a graduate of Bob Jones University and holds the D.Min. from Western Theological Seminary and the Lit.D. from Liberty University. For twenty-five years he pastored one of the nation's outstanding churches in San Diego, which grew to three locations. It was during that time that he founded two accredited Christian high schools, a Christian school system of ten schools, and Christian Heritage College.

Dr. LaHaye has written over forty books, with over eleven million copies in print in thirty-two languages. He has written books on a wide variety of subjects, such as family life, temperaments, and Bible prophecy. His current fiction works written by Jerry Jenkins—*Left Behind, Tribulation Force, Nicolae, Soul Harvest,* and *Apollyon*—have all reached number one on the Christian best-seller charts. Other works by Dr. LaHaye are *Spirit-Controlled Temperament; How to Be Happy though Married; The Act of Marriage; Revelation Unveiled, Understanding the Last Days; Rapture under Attack: Will You Escape the Tribulation?;* and the youth fiction series, Left Behind: The Kids.

He is the father of four children and grandfather of nine. Snow skiing, waterskiing, motorcycling, golfing, vacationing with family, and jogging are among his leisure activities.

The Future Is Clear

In one shocking moment, millions around the globe disappear. Those left behind face an uncertain future—especially the four kids who now find themselves alone.

Best-selling authors Jerry B. Jenkins and Tim LaHaye present the Rapture and Tribulation through the eyes of four friends—Judd, Vicki, Lionel, and Ryan. As the world falls in around them, they band together to find faith and fight the evil forces that threaten their lives.

#1: The Vanishings Four friends face Earth's last days together.

#2: Second Chance The kids search for the truth.

#3: Through the Flames The kids risk their lives.

#4: Facing the Future The kids prepare for battle.

#5: Nicolae High The Young Trib Force goes back to school.

#6: The Underground The Young Trib Force fights back.